LONG LIVE MARY, QUEEN OF SCOTS!

THE ARREST AND ESCAPE OF MARY,

QUEEN OF SCOTS

Stewart Ross

Timeliners

LONG LIVE MARY,
QUEEN OF SCOTS!

C
L
r

ReadZone Books Limited

First published in this edition 2016

© copyright in the text Stewart Ross, 1998
© copyright in this edition ReadZone Books 2016

First published 1998 by Evans Brothers Ltd

The right of the Author to be identified as the Author of this work
has been asserted by the Author in accordance with the Copyright,
Designs and Patents Act 1988.

Printed in Malta by Melita Press

Every attempt has been made by the Publisher to secure
appropriate permissions for material reproduced in this book.
If there has been any oversight we will be happy to rectify the
situation in future editions or reprints. Written submissions should
be made to the Publishers.

British Library Cataloguing in Publication Data (CIP) is available
for this title.

ISBN 978 1 78322 567 5

Visit our website: www.readzonebooks.com

CONTENTS

Page 7   **TO THE READER**

Page 8   **THE STORY SO FAR**

Page 10   **TIME LINE**

Page 13   **Chapter 1 | 'BURN HER!'**
Mary is taken to Edinburgh. The people howl at her.

Page 16   **Chapter 2 | THE PRISONER**
Mary is taken to Lochleven Castle. She is held there as
a prisoner.

Page 20   **Chapter 3 | 'PLEASE RESCUE ME!'**
Mary finds a friend but loses her babies.

Page 22   **Chapter 4 | QUEEN NO MORE**
Mary gives up the throne to her thirteen-month-old son.

Page 25   **Chapter 5 | 'YOU MUST ESCAPE!'**
Mary asks her brother to rule Scotland. She talks of escape.

Page 28   **Chapter 6 | THE LATEST LIE**
Mary's life is more comfortable. Her brother says she is
a murderer.

Page 31   **Chapter 7 | LAST CHANCE**
Mary tries to escape. The plan fails. She prepares to try again.

Page 34   **Chapter 8 | 'LONG LIVE MARY, QUEEN OF SCOTS!'**
Mary escapes and is welcomed by the people.

Page 39   **THE HISTORY FILE**

Page 43   **NEW WORDS**

TO THE READER

Long Live Mary, Queen of Scots! is a story. It is based on history. The main events in this book really happened. But some of the details, such as what people said, are made up. I hope this makes the story more fun to read. I also hope that *Long Live Mary, Queen of Scots!* will get you interested in real history. When you have finished, perhaps you will want to find out more about the sad life of Queen Mary.

Stewart Ross

THE STORY SO FAR ...

THE BABY QUEEN

Mary was born on 8th December, 1542. Her father was
King James V of Scotland. Her mother was a French lady.
King James died eight days later, so Mary became queen
of Scotland while still a tiny baby.

As Scotland was very troubled, Mary was sent to
France for her safety. She grew into a beautiful, lively
young woman. But she was very spoilt. In 1558 she
married Francis, a French prince.

QUEEN MARY

The next year Francis became king of France. Mary was
now queen of Scotland and France. Sadly, her young
husband died in 1560. There was now no reason for
Mary to stay in France. At the age of eighteen, she came
back to Scotland.

The Scottish people adored their charming young
queen. Her court was full of music and fun. In 1565 she
married her cousin, Lord Darnley, and at first the couple
were very happy.

THINGS GO WRONG

Mary did not rule wisely. Worse still, she stopped loving
Lord Darnley and grew friendly with other men. Many
Scottish lords began to get annoyed with her.

In 1566 Mary had a son, Prince James.

Soon afterwards, early in 1567, Lord Darnley was murdered. Only three months later, Mary married James, Earl of Bothwell. The other lords were furious and gathered an army.

Mary and Bothwell called up their troops. They went to meet the rebels near Edinburgh. When the queen's soldiers refused to fight, Bothwell said he was going to get help …

TIME LINE
CE (Common Era)

1542
8 December Mary born in Linlithgow, Scotland
14 December Mary's father, King James V, dies

1548
Mary sent to France

1559
Francis becomes king of France

1560
Francis dies

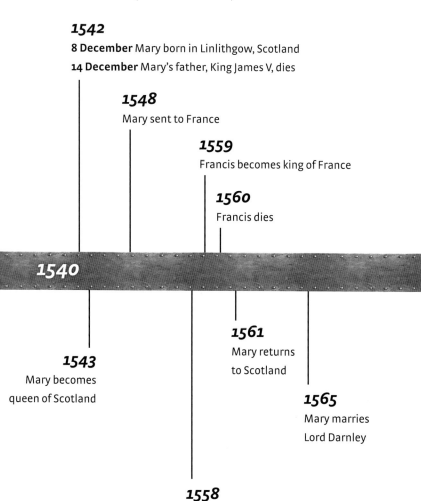

1540

1543
Mary becomes
queen of Scotland

1561
Mary returns
to Scotland

1565
Mary marries
Lord Darnley

1558
Mary marries the French prince, Francis.
Elizabeth, Mary's cousin, becomes queen of
England

1566
19 June Prince James born

1568
2 May Mary escapes from Lochleven Castle
13 May The rebels defeat Mary at Langside
17 May Mary arrives in England

1603
Queen Elizabeth I dies. James becomes King James I of England

1603

1587
Mary executed at Fotheringhay, England

1567
10 February Lord Darnley murdered
15 May Mary marries James, Earl of Bothwell
15 June Mary surrenders to the rebel lords
17 June Mary taken to Lochleven Castle
24 July James becomes King James VI of Scotland

Chapter 1

'BURN HER!'

Queen Mary held her husband tight. 'Dear James, come back soon. Please!' she begged.

'Don't worry, my love', he said. 'Be strong and brave, for Scotland's sake. I will return soon with an army big enough to make you queen of the whole world!'

Mary tried to laugh. 'You always look on the bright side, don't you James?'

James, Earl of Bothwell, took his arms from round her neck. 'Of course I look on the bright side!' He smiled. 'What other side is there?'

The queen shook her head. 'There is a dark side, James, full of pain and unhappiness. I am afraid of it.'

He gave her hand a squeeze. 'Come on! There's no point thinking like that! Go and talk to the rebels. Keep them happy until I come back with my army. Then we'll rule together in peace for the rest of our lives.'

Mary laid a hand on her stomach. 'And our baby?' she asked.

'When our child is born, it will be the merriest wee baby in all Scotland', he laughed. 'It will have brothers and sisters, too – dozens of them! Just you wait and see!'

He turned and walked quickly towards his horse. 'Farewell, my beautiful queen', he called. 'And don't worry!'

With a heavy heart, Mary watched James jump into the saddle and gallop away towards the setting sun.

When he had gone, she went back to her soldiers. Then minutes later she rode down the hill to meet the rebels.

Even before she reached the rebel camp, Mary realised something was wrong. She was not cheered, as she once had been. Some of the men jeered and whistled at her. One or two shouted rude remarks. But it was too late to turn back now.

She rode straight up to the rebel leader, Lord Morton. 'I have kept my word, Morton', she said. 'My husband has gone and I have come to talk with you.' Although she was tired and worried, she did her best to sound brave.

Morton's face was pale and hard. 'Thank you, madam', he said coldly.

Mary shuddered at his words. A queen was normally called 'Your Grace', not 'madam'. She bit her lip. 'Morton', she said as calmly as she could, 'Remind your men that I am their queen. Tell them to hold their rude tongues'.

Morton stared at her with eyes of ice. 'I cannot command my men's hearts', he replied. 'They speak out of anger.'

The queen suddenly felt terribly lonely. 'Oh James!' she whispered. 'I need you. Please come back!'

'Now, madam', barked Morton, 'Be so good as to follow me.'

'Where are we going?' Mary asked.

'Edinburgh.'

'To my palace?' Mary longed to change her dress and have a good meal.

'Palace?' sneered Morton. 'We'll find a room. But it won't be a palace.'

The journey back to the city was like a nightmare. Yelling crowds lined the road. 'Burn her!' they screamed. 'Kill her! The witch must die!'

Tears streamed down Mary's face. Her fine clothes were crumpled and muddy. She was faint from hunger. Two burly soldiers rode beside her. There was no escape.

They took the queen to the house of one of her enemies and locked her in an upstairs room. She went to the window and looked out. Before her hung a white banner. On it was painted the bloody body of Lord Darnley. Mary let out a cry of horror and collapsed to the floor.

Chapter 2

THE PRISONER

After another horrible day, Mary was taken to her palace. At last she was among friends. Her ladies were shocked to see her to pale and ill. Her clothes were torn and her lovely red hair was in a terrible mess.

After the queen had washed and changed her dress, she felt much better. She sat down to a hearty supper. It was the first food she had eaten for more than a day.

Morton stood behind her chair as she ate. He wanted to make sure she did not get up to any tricks. When she had finished her soup. Mary turned to him. 'Morton, why are you treating me like this?' she asked.

The earl said nothing.

'I came to you willingly', Mary went on. 'To help you find who killed Lord Darnley.' Again, the earl said nothing.

Mary picked up a piece of chicken. 'Is my son safe?' she asked.

'He's in Stirling Castle', Morton replied. 'Safe from all murderers.'

Mary pretended not to hear. 'I will remain here', she went on, 'with my ladies. Please bring my son to me.'

Morton snorted. 'Not a chance, madam. You'll—'. He stopped as a messenger came in and spoke to him. 'Right!' he said when the man had gone. 'Time to leave.'

Mary threw down her knife. 'Leave!' she cried. 'I shall not! I'll not be ordered about like this!'

'Oh yes?' sneered Morton. 'Guards!' Two soldiers stepped forward. One put a hand on the queen's shoulder.

'Don't touch me!' she screamed. 'I am still a queen and I shall guide my own footsteps.'

Mary was allowed to take only two maids with her. The rest of her ladies began to wail and sob. Morton was annoyed. 'Shut up!' he shouted. He glared at Mary. 'Get a move on!'

'I haven't got my clothes yet', she answered.

'You won't need any!'

Mary looked at him carefully. 'Are we going to Stirling, to see my son?'

Morton turned away. 'Maybe. Now hurry up!'

The queen was led to a horse waiting outside. The small group rode swiftly through the dark streets of the city and headed north. Mary's heart leaped with joy. This was the way to Stirling! Soon she would see her baby son again. She was wrong. They turned off the main road and followed narrow lanes lined with trees. After several hours they came to a loch. A boat was waiting for them.

Mary looked around. Behind her loomed the shapes of houses. In the distance, across the dark water, a light shone. She had been here before, she remembered, in happier times.

Loch Leven! The light shone from a castle on a small island in the middle of the loch.

It was a grim place, ideal for a prison.

The queen was rowed across the smooth black water to the island. When she arrived, she was taken to a small room in the castle tower. She said goodnight to her maids and lay down on the narrow bed.

All was dark and still. The only sounds were the muttering of the guards and lapping of the waves on the shore. Mary, queen of Scotland, was a prisoner in her own country.

She got up and knelt beside the bed to pray. 'Help me, O God!' she sobbed. 'Look after my baby son. Guard my husband James. May he come quickly and take me from this terrible place!'

Chapter 3

'PLEASE RESCUE ME!'

Mary spent her first two weeks at the castle in bed. She was sick and miserable. Everything she loved had been taken from her. There was no news from her husband. Her baby was many kilometres away, in the hands of her enemies. She had hardly any clothes and almost none of her jewels.

To make matters worse, she had few friends about her. Her maids were too frightened to help. The guards and servants hardly spoke to her. Sir William Douglas, the lord of the castle, was as hard as the stones in the tower. His mother, the Old Lady, seemed to think Mary was a witch. Nothing good could come of a pretty girl brought up in France, she said. Especially if she had red hair.

Sir William made sure Mary was never left alone. The eyes of Drysdale, the chief guard, followed her wherever she went. On most nights Sir William's wife slept in the queen's room.

In time, however, Mary's health returned. The colour came back to her cheeks and she was strong enough to take walks round the island. As she got better, she cheered up. She took more care with the clothes and hair. Slowly, day by day, her magical charm returned.

Two young men noticed the change in the beautiful queen. Before long they were both under her spell. Geordie Douglas, the handsome younger brother of Sir William, gazed at Mary with eyes full of wonder. But he was afraid to say anything. The dashing Lord Ruthven was more daring.

One morning he burst into Mary's room and threw himself at her feet. 'Oh you angel!' he cried. 'You cannot know how much I love you! Do you love me? Say you do! Please say you do!'

Mary did not know quite what to say. She loved it when men worshipped her like this. But she had a husband and was expecting his baby.

'My dear Ruthven', she said quietly, 'Please get up.' She put out a hand and lifted him to his feet. 'Now listen. I am very fond of you. You have been a good friend and have helped me a lot. But you cannot speak to me like this. I am a married woman and ...'.

'But I cannot live without you', wailed Ruthven. 'Please say you love me!'

Mary shook her head. 'No, I cannot. Please leave me. If you stay here, we'll both get into trouble.'

Ruthven gave her one last loving look, then walked from the room. A week later he was told to leave the island.

Geordie was not surprised when Ruthven went. 'He was in love with you', he said to Mary. They were walking together in the castle garden.

'I know', Mary replied. 'Poor man!'

Geordie sighed. 'I don't blame him, Your Grace. You are like a ray of sunshine in this miserable dump. Your smile brightens up the whole place.'

Mary stopped and looked at him. 'Thank you, Geordie. You are a friend I can trust, aren't you?'

The young man blushed. 'You can trust me with your life', he whispered.

A few days afterwards, Mary fell sick again with a fever. The illness put a great strain on her. Her pregnancy ended too soon, and her unborn babies died. (Mary learned that she had lost not one child, but twins.)

'What can I do?' she wept. 'I have lost my husband and my son, and now I have lost my babies! Rescue me, someone! Oh please rescue me!'

Chapter 4

QUEEN NO MORE

Mary's illness left her weak and sadder than ever. There was no news from her husband and no one came to rescue her. But she did have a visitor.

It was Lindsay, one of the rebel lords. He marched into her room, carrying a bundle of papers. 'Good morning, madam', he said quickly. 'I'm glad to see you are better.'

Mary could not believe her ears. 'Better?' she gasped. 'Lord Lindsay, I am still very sick.'

He put his papers on the table and looked across to where she was sitting. 'Well enough to get out of bed', he said. 'So well enough to sign these.' He tapped the papers with his finger.

'What are they?'

'Papers, madam.'

Mary glanced angrily at him. 'I am not stupid, Lindsay. What do you want me to sign?'

He handed her one of the papers. 'Put your name on this, and I will leave you in peace.'

As she read what was written, Mary began to shake. 'Never!' she gasped.

'What was that?'

'I said, Lindsay, that I will never sign this. You want me to give up my crown.'

Lindsay sat on the windowsill. 'Not really. We want you to give the crown to your son. Because you're a prisoner, it's not really yours anymore.'

'How dare you!' Mary shouted. She tried to stand up but was too weak.

Lindsay looked at her, then at the loch. 'I hear the water's very deep', he said slowly.

'What do you mean?' Mary said anxiously.

'Dear me! Don't you understand, madam? I mean that if you fell into the water – by accident, of course – you would drown.'

Mary stared at him in horror. Later that day she signed the papers. Her son was now king of Scotland.

One afternoon in late July, Mary heard the castle guns firing. She went outside to see what was happening. Bonfires were burning in the garden. Sir William and Drysdale were drinking and laughing.

Mary asked what was going on. 'We're holding a coronation party', Drysdale grinned. He offered Mary a cup of wine. 'Come and join us!'

Mary pushed the cup aside. 'You're doing what?' she cried.

Sir William explained. 'We're celebrating the king's coronation. He's your son. Aren't you happy for him?'

Tears sprang from Mary's eyes. 'How could you be so cruel?' she wept. Without another word, she ran back into the castle.

Mary sat by the window while her maid did her hair. It was towards the end of summer and the trees on the island were edged with gold. It's strange, she thought, how even a prison can look beautiful sometimes.

A large boat was crossing the loch towards the castle. Mary watched it carefully. One of the men in the boat looked familiar. Just before it reached the shore, she suddenly jumped up.

'Look!' she cried. 'How wonderful!'

The maid put down her comb and peered out of the window. 'What is it, my lady?'

'It's my brother, Lord Moray. He must have returned from abroad. Now he's come to see me. A rescuer, at last!'

Mary quickly tidied herself up and ran down to the shore. 'Brother! Brother!' she shouted, waving her arms. Lord Moray looked up. He did not wave back.

As he stood up to get out of the boat, Mary noticed a strange look in his eye. Something else worried her, too. The boatmen called him 'Your Grace'.

Chapter 5

'YOU MUST ESCAPE!'

As soon as her brother was on shore, Mary rushed up him and kissed him. 'I'm so glad you've come!' she cried.

Moray stepped back awkwardly. 'I am pleased to see you, sister', he said. His voice sounded tight and frosty. 'But please don't kiss me.'

Mary laughed. 'Not kiss my own brother? Don't be silly!'

'Don't laugh at me, Mary!' Moray barked. 'We all know how you use your charm to get what you want. Well, it will not work with me. Take me inside. We need to talk.'

Mary followed him into the castle. He's only pretending, she thought. He'll change when we're alone. I know he will.

But Moray did not change. His love for his sister had shrivelled away. When they were alone, he was even more unkind to her than he had been outside.

'You are a disgrace!' he shouted. 'First you were a lousy queen. Then you were friendly with unsuitable people. Then you allowed poor Lord Darnley to be murdered. Then, worst of all, you went and married that scoundrel Bothwell only days afterwards! Don't you ever think, woman? Can't you guess what everyone is saying about you?'

Mary covered her face with her hands. 'You are too hard, brother', she sobbed. 'I thought you loved me!'

Moray paced up and down the room. 'Love you? Yes, I loved you once. But you have ruined everything. There are times now when all I want to do is cut your throat!'

Moray stayed for two days. He spent much of the time with Mary, bullying her, shouting at her, threatening her. In the end, she began to believe what he said.

'You have been a fool, haven't you, Mary?' he asked.

'Yes!' she replied weakly. 'I have done awful things.' Her face was swollen with crying.

'So what is to be done?'

Mary stared at him with red, tired eyes. 'You must rule Scotland, dear brother. Until the king is old enough to rule for himself.'

'Is that what you want?'

'Yes!' Mary begged. 'Please rule for my son. Please. I am not fit to do so.'

A smile spread over Moray's face. 'Very well. I will do as you ask. I shall rule Scotland. As for you, Mary, I suggest you spend the rest of your life asking God to forgive you.'

Mary sank to her knees. 'Yes. Thank you brother. I shall ask God for forgiveness.'

In the weeks that followed, Mary thought about what her brother had done. She saw how he had cruelly forced her to agree with his plans. She would never forgive him.

To make matters worse, she heard bad news of her husband. He had not raised an army. Instead, he had been chased out of the country. There was little chance that he would ever return.

'So you see', she said to Geordie one evening, 'I have no friends left'.

The young man checked that the guards were not listening. 'That's not true, Your Grace!' he said fiercely. 'Most of Scotland still thinks of you as their queen.'

'Most of Scotland?'

'Well, most of the people I speak to.'

Mary gazed across the loch. 'What's the good of that?' she asked. 'Who wants a queen stuck on an island?'

Geordie glanced around nervously.
'You don't have to stay here', he whispered.

'You mean … ?'

'Of course! You must escape!'

Mary's eyes blazed with excitement. 'You'll help me?' she asked.

Geordie blushed. 'Don't you remember what I once said? You can trust me with your life.'

Chapter 6

THE LATEST LIE

Geordie wanted Mary to try and escape at once.
At first she agreed. But after thinking it over, she
changed her mind. It was best to wait a bit, she decided.
Now her husband had gone and her son was king, the
lords might set her free. She might even be rescued by
soldiers from France.

Escape was a big risk. If the lords caught her, they
would lock her behind bars – or kill her. While she was
safe on the island, she would stay there.

Things got better that autumn. Mary felt healthier
than she had done for a long time. The lords allowed
her more clothes and servants. Friends sent her gifts.
Geordie paid the boatman to smuggle letters for her.
Best of all, she was joined by her great friend, Mary
Seton.

There was, however, one piece of bad news.
Sir William sent for Mary one wet afternoon in late
September. She found him in his private rooms, reading
a letter.

'I have something important to tell you, madam',
he said. 'You had better sit down.'

Mary took a chair by the fire. 'I have received a letter
from Lord Moray', Sir William went on. 'He says he has
good news from Denmark.'

Mary looked up. Sir William added, 'But I don't think you'll find it good'.

'Go on', said Mary quietly.

'Your husband, Lord Bothwell, has been captured. He is in prison.'

'Prison?'

'Actually, he's in a dungeon. In chains. You'll never see him again.'

Mary stood up. 'Thank you for telling me. But you were right – I don't think it's good news. It's tragic. I hope the poor man will not be cruelly treated.'

Back in her own rooms, Mary prayed for her husband. She also asked God for strength to continue her struggle alone.

Autumn slipped into winter. Icy winds blew across the dark waters of the loch and howled around the castle's grim walls. Mary spent most of her time indoors. She was in good spirits.

The days were filled with games and laughter. At night the grey towers echoed to the sounds of dancing. Mary saw a lot of Geordie and their friendship grew. In shadowy corners the servants whispered of romance. Sir William heard the gossip with a face like thunder.

Just before Christmas, Geordie found Mary looking through the window at the distant shore. 'Do I really have friends out there?' she asked.

'Thousands and thousands, Your Grace', he replied. 'All waiting for you.'

She turned back into the room. 'Then why am I still here? What excuse does my brother give for keeping me a prisoner?'

Geordie looked serious. 'He is afraid of the love the people have for you, Your Grace. He does all he can to blacken your name.'

Mary sat at the table and took up her sewing. 'What's his latest lie?'

'Do you really want to know, Your Grace?'

'Of course. Is it so bad?'

'Well', said Geordie, 'He says that you plotted with the Earl of Bothwell'.

'To do what?' Mary asked, although she knew the answer.

'To murder Lord Darnley, Your Grace.'

Mary put down her sewing. 'You know that is not true, don't you, Geordie?'

'It is a damned lie!'

Mary smiled at him. 'Of course. But it means I am in great danger. The rebels may put me on trial for murder.'

Geordie leant across the table. 'Then you know what you must do, Your Grace, don't you?'

'Yes, Geordie. I think the time has come to plan my escape.'

Chapter 7

LAST CHANCE

Sir William was worried.

The whole island seemed under Mary's spell.
Sir William could trust no one, apart from himself and
Drysdale. The women hero-worshipped his beautiful
prisoner. Even the Old Lady spoke kindly to her.
The men treated her like a goddess. Geordie followed
her about like a lovesick puppy. The guards blushed
when she spoke to them.

Sir William had to do something. Several times he
told Geordie to leave Mary alone. The young man took
no notice. Finally, in the spring, the two men had a
quarrel, and Geordie was ordered off the island.

Mary was very upset at the news. But Geordie was
not dismayed. He would arrange her escape from
the other side of the loch, he said. Willie Douglas, an
orphaned cousin living at the castle, would also help.
Geordie gave him gold to smuggle Mary's letters.
The money was not needed. Willie was as crazy about
Mary as Geordie was.

The first plan went wrong. Mary Seton stayed
in Mary's rooms, pretending to be her mistress.
Meanwhile, Mary dressed as a washerwoman and
covered her face with a shawl.

Without anyone noticing, she walked from the castle

and got into a boat going to the mainland.

The boatman stared at the strange young woman. He had never seen her before and she looked rather nice. 'Let's see your face, lassie', he asked. Mary refused. He leaned forward to pull off her shawl. Mary lifted a hand to stop him.

The boatman gasped. The hand was smooth and white. The passenger was no washerwoman! Mary begged him not to give her away. He agreed, but refused to ferry her across the loch.

Mary retuned to the castle and told Mary Seton what had happened. 'Don't worry, Your Grace', she said cheerfully. 'At least the man kept your secret. You'll get away next time, I'm sure you will.'

Later, Mary had another narrow escape. Sir William's young daughter saw Willie carrying secret letters to Mary. The girl was terrified. What should she do? Tell her father or keep quiet?

Mary had a long talk with her. The prisoner's charm worked like magic, and the girl promised not to say anything.

Sir William's wife was expecting a baby at the end of April. For several weeks she would not be sleeping in Mary's room. This was the chance Mary had been waiting for. But somehow she had to tell her friends on the mainland.

Geordie pretended to his family that he was going abroad. The Old Lady was horrified and begged him not to go.

He refused. In despair, the Old Lady asked Mary to write to him and ask him to stay. Of course, she agreed.

Mary hid a note in her letter, telling Geordie that now was the time to escape. Before long a message came back. Everything was prepared. Lord Seton and other friends of Mary's were ready to welcome her. All she had to do now was get off the island.

Mary and Willie discussed plans. He suggested she could leap off the castle wall and run to a boat. Mary was not so sure. She got one of her maids to try the jump, to see if it was possible. The girl twisted her ankle when she landed and the plan was dropped. Mary had to rely on disguise again.

Willie had a new idea. He arranged a spring pageant for 2nd May. The whole castle would join in. Mary would be able to escape during the excitement, he promised.

It was her last chance.

Chapter 8

LONG LIVE MARY, QUEEN OF SCOTS!

The pageant was a great success. Willie took the lead.
All morning he danced about the island, pretending to be
drunk. Laughing, Mary and her ladies followed.
After lunch Mary went to lie down.

In the afternoon the Old Lady and Sir William came
to visit her. As they were talking, the Old Lady noticed a
group of horsemen on the mainland. They were Mary's
supporters gathering to greet her. Mary was terrified.
To stop the Old Lady thinking about what was
happening, Mary started shouting about her brother.

Then Sir William looked out of the window.
He noticed Willie making holes in the boats. This was
to stop the guards following Mary when she got away.
'What on earth's the boy doing?' he grumbled.

Once again Mary had to think fast. She pretended to
faint and Sir William went to fetch her a glass of wine.
He forgot about the boats.

Later Mary got into one of her maid's dresses and put
one of her own over the top. As usual, Sir William brought
her supper. Afterwards, he went to have his own meal,
and Drysdale went off to play hand ball.

Everything was now ready.

Mary slipped off her own dress and covered her head
with a hood.

Willie stole Sir William's keys while he was having supper. He signalled to Mary to get going.

He opened the gate. Mary walked straight across the courtyard and out of the castle. Willie locked the gate and threw away the keys. The couple walked quickly down to a boat and got in.

'Oh look!' called out a washerwoman standing nearby. 'It's the prisoner!'

Willie glared at her. 'Shut up, woman!' he hissed.

Seconds later the boat was heading across the loch for the distant shore. At last, Mary was free!

Geordie was waiting for Mary when she came ashore. 'Welcome to freedom, Your Grace!' he cried, kneeling at her feet.

'Thank you, Geordie', she replied warmly. Taking his hand, she added, 'I knew you would not let me down'.

There was no time to be lost. Two fine horses were waiting, stolen from Sir William's stables.

Mary and Willie mounted them and rode fast for Lord Seton's castle at Niddry. The country people cheered as she galloped by.

They reached Niddry at midnight. Mary was tired out. After a light meal, she went straight to bed.

The next morning, Mary was woken by shouting. When she first opened her eyes, she could not remember where she was. Was she back in Edinburgh? Was that the mob she could hear, yelling for her life?

She got dressed quickly. She did not even do her hair, but left it waving over her shoulders.

The shouting grew louder.

By the door she asked a guard what the noise was. 'The people, Your Grace', he replied with a bow.

'What do they want?'

'I think they want you, Your Grace. They are calling for their queen.' He threw open the door and Mary walked outside.

A huge crowd had gathered outside the castle. When they saw Mary, they let out a great cheer. 'Long live Mary, Queen of Scots!' they yelled.

Mary raised her hand and waved. 'Thank you', she called. 'Thank you, my dear people!' She turned to find Willie by her side. 'I am a queen again', she smiled. 'Thanks be to God!'

Willie smiled back at her. 'Your Grace, in the hearts of true Scots, you have always been their queen. And you always will be.'

THE HISTORY FILE

WHAT HAPPENED NEXT?

Disaster

When he learned his prisoner had got away, Sir William was so upset that he tried to kill himself. Meanwhile, Mary was planning to take on the rebels. Many men joined her army. On 13 May, eleven days after her escape, they fought the rebels at the Battle of Langside.

Mary's army lost the battle. She managed to escape into England. Elizabeth, queen of England, was Mary's cousin. Mary hoped she would help her.

A prisoner in England

Elizabeth was not sure what to do. She was a Protestant. Mary was a Catholic. Many Catholics said England should not have a Protestant queen. They wanted Mary to be queen of England instead of Elizabeth. This made Mary a danger to Elizabeth.

Elizabeth held meetings to hear what Mary had to say for herself. Nothing was decided. To try and stop Mary making trouble, Elizabeth kept her a prisoner in castles and country houses. Geordie and Willie Douglas stayed with her, but she did not marry again.

Execution

As we know, Mary did not like being a prisoner. She plotted and wrote secret letters asking for help. Sometimes she said she should be queen of both England and Scotland. This annoyed Elizabeth greatly.

In the end, Elizabeth had had enough. It was proved that Mary Queen of Scots had plotted to get rid of Elizabeth. Her head was cut off at Fotheringhay Castle on 8 February 1587. All over Europe Catholics complained bitterly.

Meanwhile, Mary's son James had grown into an able king. He ruled Scotland well and settled the country down after all the troubles of Mary's reign.

Queen Elizabeth did not marry and had no children. So when she died in 1603, King James became king of England as well as Scotland. The two countries have had the same king or queen ever since.

HOW DO WE KNOW?

Mary Queen of Scots is one of the most famous people in our history. People argued about her when she was alive, and they have gone on arguing about her ever since. Some say she was almost a saint. Others say she was a silly, dangerous woman who deserved to die.

Many of Mary's letters and papers have been kept. The best known are eight letters she was supposed to have written to Bothwell. They were found in a casket (a type of box) and are called the 'Casket Letters'. Moray showed them to Queen Elizabeth. He said they proved Mary played a part in Lord Darnley's murder. But we can't be sure they were really written by Mary.

Books written in Mary's time are difficult to read. The handwriting is even harder! The spelling is unusual, too. For example, Mary spelt her name 'Marie'.

Don't worry! There are lots of modern children's books on Mary and Elizabeth. See what there is in your school or town library. Perhaps you can find a picture of Mary painted when she was alive. (There were no cameras then.) I wonder if you will find her beautiful? When you are older, you could read Antonia Fraser's huge book *Mary Queen of Scots*. It's full of interesting details. In the meantime, you may be lucky enough to visit Fotheringhay Castle, Lochleven Castle, or one of the many places where Mary stayed when she was Queen of Scots.

NEW WORDS

Arrest
To make someone a prisoner.

Banner
Flag.

Boatman
A man who rows boats for his job.

Burly
Big and strong.

Coronation
When a king or queen is crowned.

Dashing
Good-looking and lively.

Earl
A nobleman.

Execution
Killing someone for breaking the law.

Jeer
To mock rudely.

Loch
A Scottish lake.

Mainland
Land that is not an island.

Mob
A crowd.

Nightmare
A bad dream.

Pageant
A big, open-air, dressing-up party.

Rebel
Someone who fights against the ruler.

Washerwoman
A woman who does other people's washing.

Your Grace
How Scots addressed someone royal.

WHAT IF THE BOMB GOES OFF?

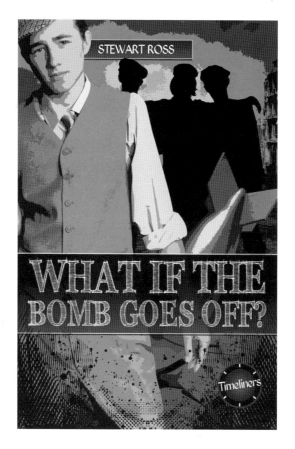

Bill, Paul, Dennis and Charlie are the Radford Road
Gang. When Bill suggests a Special Mission to hunt
for spies, the others join in - for a bit of a laugh.
But when two of them are trapped beside an
enormous unexploded bomb, the Mission becomes
deadly serious.

TIMELINERS
BRING HISTORY ALIVE!

978-1-78322-549-1

978-1-78322-559-0

978-1-78322-560-6

978-1-78322-547-7

978-1-78322-548-4

978-1-78322-567-5

978-1-78322-565-1

978-1-78322-566-8

978-1-78322-561-3

978-1-78322-537-8

978-1-78322-568-2

978-1-78322-592-7

978-1-78322-593-4

This series by Stewart Ross really sends the reader back into history! Each exciting book brings the past alive by linking key events to a fast-moving narrative.